Advance praise for

THE THEME OF TONIGHT'S PARTY HAS BEEN ~~CHANGED~~

"Dana Roeser is an aficionado of fear. Radical anxiety flows into every corner of experience for this poet, and becomes a lifestyle. Desperation is daily. 'I // wake in the dark / trying to assemble // a lexicon, / to make a coherent // line—in the dark / I scratched // words on top of each / other on a // pad by the bed / "Torture, / torture, torture." At the time / I thought it // brilliant.' If you find that passage thrillingly alive and nervy and funny and scary, then Dana Roeser is a poet for you to check out. She's no smoothie, and no chicken-disjunctivist. She is an existential protester." —MARK HALLIDAY

"From Mass to 12-step meetings, voodoo dolls to rosary beads, the poems in Dana Roeser's *The Theme of Tonight's Party Has Been Changed* are concerned finally with 'the corporeal self'— vulnerable and resilient. Roeser is a poet of fierce intelligence and high creative metabolism, and there is unmistakable urgency in these narratives, the poems' structures expansive, 'stealthy, labyrinthine,' and irresistible." —CLAUDIA EMERSON

"What I love about Dana Roeser's poems is the way they unfold— beginning with the first glimpse; their formal or 'razored' look on the page—and how these energetic narratives split into complexities of rhetoric and landscape—fictions full of characters the poet presents in a full-blown orchestration of the self that is anything but ordinary or self-indulgent. Halfway through a typical Roeser poem I find my breathing has been changed—I'm that caught up in the performance and the story. There is a plushly confessional core to the poems, and yet the self-deprecating humor and the velocity—I'd call this Roeser's Voice—save them from any possibility of bathos. Instead, I end up feeling moved beyond measure by this poet's spirit, as reflected in the poems, in the face of failures and unrelenting desire. A lyric poet who writes narrative poems, Dana Roeser is a poet who transcends classification." —DAVID DODD LEE

THE THEME OF TONIGHT'S PARTY HAS BEEN CHANGED

———

THE THEME OF TONIGHT'S PARTY HAS BEEN CHANGED

Poems

Dana Roeser

UNIVERSITY OF MASSACHUSETTS PRESS

Amherst and Boston

Copyright © 2014 by Dana Roeser
All rights reserved
Printed in the United States of America

ISBN 978-1-62534-097-9 (pbk)
Set in Monotype Apollo
Printed and bound by IBT Hamilton, Inc.

Library of Congress Cataloging-in-Publication Data

Roeser, Dana, 1953– author.
[Poems. Selections]
The theme of tonight's party has been changed : poems / Dana Roeser.
pages cm
ISBN 978-1-62534-097-9 (pbk. : alk. paper)
I. Title.
PS3618.O38A6 2014
811'.6—dc23
2013051027

British Library Cataloguing-in-Publication Data
A catalogue record for this book is available from the British Library.

For Don, Eleanor, and Lucy
For my father

CONTENTS

THE THEME OF TONIGHT'S PARTY HAS BEEN CHANGED

DELIVER US FROM EVIL

—

Do you reject the glamour of evil, and refuse to be mastered by sin?

Baptismal promise

Goats and monkeys
I'm just a messed-up
person trying to live

on a spiritual basis.
Every thought I have I have to
discard. "This is projection."

"This is the ugliest
tackiest in the most poor
taste book cover I

ever saw and they're doing it
to humiliate me." "This is
False Evidence Appearing

Real." My daughter's boyfriend
is a spider in its web
waiting in the South of France

to drug her and eat her
like a limp fly. Goats and monkeys.
Othello's mind was

infected. Lord deliver me
from my dreams. "My old high
school girlfriend

stabbing a friend
with a pair of scissors and me
facing time for

seeing it," Jay
confided. Or "I lay
down to go to sleep

at 11:30
and regretted I hadn't
rammed the guy who

boxed me in on
the highway, that I hadn't pummeled
his car with eggs." This from

the cute put-together
blonde. When the past is guilt
and remorse

and the future is fear. "The past
is history. The future
is a mystery. Today is all we

have. That's why
they call it the present." "Naked
in bed, Iago, and not mean

harm?" That my daughter will
somehow live the Othello
story, that her love is

too perfect, I mean her *drug,*
I mean her *love.* "Every thought
had to be discarded."

"They that mean virtuously,
and yet do so, / The devil their virtue
tempts, and they tempt

heaven." I said at dinner,
"Don't you look
at every endorsement for its

double meaning—like
if it says 'She has
a good eye,' it means

'She has a rotten ear'?" Richard
and Adam just looked
              at me dumbfounded. Goats and

                    monkeys. Magic magnifying
mind, John said,
              ten years ago in Carrollton. He'd

                    driven drunk on
a fake license and been sent
              to prison again. Eleanor said

                    The Dark Knight is all
about the power of evil,
              having those thoughts

                    planted. In the minds
of a whole city. "I'll chop her into messes—
              cuckhold me!" "That's

                    the last thing I need,"
she said, after her second
              time watching.

                    Everyone knows the actor
who played the
              evil "doer" ended

                    up killing himself with drugs
after finishing that role. "The role
              of his life." Everyone

                    says, "Oh no, those rumors
aren't true, about him
              being haunted. . . ." He

                    didn't sleep for *how*
long? He took *what* drugs, in combination
              with *what* meds?

             I paced myself,
I walked I ran I kept a
             routine. And coached my daughter

             over the phone to do
another version of the same. "I lost my
             job because I'm a loser." That

             snippet danced in the
shower with me under the faulty
             showerhead

             put there
so that my hair
             would always have a filthy

             residue. "A raven o'er
the infected house, / Boding to all—
             he had my handkerchief."

             "Uncover, discover, discard."
Finally the truth of it,
             every thought

             had to be discarded. "No
romancing it." "Move a muscle. Change a
             thought." Rejecting

             every thought. "When I started
making excuses, I started
             noticing the voice

             wasn't mine." "That's bullshit."
"That's projection." "That's "F.E.A.R."
             That's "recycling," "relapse,"

             "Old Behavior." "Whose
voice *was* that?" Stinking
             thinking. "Evil stuff

came into my head." "Handkerchief—
confessions—handkerchief."
          "Gratitude

               is an action." "I haven 't
smoked cigarettes
          in twelve days. Yesterday

               I really wanted to." Black-wavy-
haired Celeste, holding
          her child

               on her lap, "I wanted
to fly off the planet . . . blue skies
          forever." "Strumpet, I know

               it was irrational." "See
it the way it is." Goats and monkeys. He
          grabbed his wife

               by the neck
and squeezed. "She sang
          a song about a willow."

GENIUS OF THE PRAIRIE:
BENTON COUNTY WIND FARM

—

Noon meeting, UU Church

It was a bad
        day we didn't
know why
        we hated ourselves.
Betsy said she had
        to keep reminding
herself, "Principles
        above personalities."
She said she hated
        Twelve-Step show-offs.
Mike said he couldn't
        stand the meetings
where he was being
        talked *at*. Also,
that in the last few
        days he'd decided
he was a bad teacher,
        a bad student, his
house was a mess, and he
        wasn't a good
friend. I said I didn't
        trust anybody's
motives, especially the
        normies', and then
that I hated how people
        kept disappearing
from meetings, and then
        finally how I didn't
trust my motives either—come
        to think of it,
I could certainly see
        why my family
called me self-righteous
        and sanctimonious. Jenny
said she was at first

          so ashamed
she certainly
          was *not* going to
let anybody know
          she was a member. Then
how even now she wasn't
          thrilled about having
it broadcast. We all talked
          about the movie
I missed, because I don't have
          cable, about Lois and
Bill Wilson, and I said, Bill
          certainly was screwed-up
himself wasn't he and how
          reassuring that was. Jason was
called on and refused
          to speak but then
after somebody else shared
          he spoke
up. Carleton said he was
          just trying to
get back into reality. Finally
          Max said he'd
said goodbye to his mom
          yesterday as though
he were going to the noon
          meeting—and he
did not go. He drove right past
          and up into the wind
farms in Benton
          County. Even before
he said anything more,
          I remembered
the day Mia drove
          to the wind farms, off
of 65, leaving
          everything. Madia
and Alicia (whom Madia
          wasn't too crazy about,
given the fact A.

was—and is—on opiates)
drove north too
          and on a hunch pulled
into the first wind farm visible
          from the interstate.
They found Mia curled up in
          a hidden cul-de-sac,
parked. It all seemed like
          such a performance
except M. really was
          miserable and really would
have offed herself. Left
          her young children, stoned
Alicia, sponsee Madia,
          and me. Max
drove back
          south and to Hort Park
for some reason, pulled
          over, slept for six
hours. Then got
          up to complete
his plan. He started driving
          again, but then
drove right past the place
          he'd decided to do
it. Every terrible, negative
          thing he said to himself,
some lovely bromide from one
          of the meetings
or the Big Book
          rejoined. Tit
for tat, his mind
          was busy. Finally,
he went home and told
          his parents how infantilizing
it was for them
          to question
him all the time, how
          ashamed
they had made him feel

hassling him
about money and his lack
of responsibility regarding
same (when he was trying
to get ready to
take finals). He felt better
enough to go to bed
and then showed up at the meeting
today.
The weather
was chalky and irritatingly
the blinds
were shut opaque
down to the place
where the windows
could be opened (though it
was too cold
to do so). I thought,
as I often do in that
room, For God's sakes
we need
light. But I didn't get
up and yank the metal blinds
as I sometimes
do. I was too depressed and
didn't trust myself. C.
touched my hand twice passing
the 12 and 12
back and forth and that
set me spinning. And
again for the final
prayer. I wasn't
there for what seemed like
might have been
the final squeeze—
I'd pulled my
hand away. The wind
farms look more
high-tech than the
windmills did in

the South of France. Each turbine
          is metal, over
three hundred feet tall,
          with three swooping
Brancusi-looking
          arms. Slim, like
birds in flight, that's what they
          were called in the
Atelier Brancusi
          at the foot of the
Centre Georges
          Pompidou. Once one
started looking through the
          glass into the sculptor's
recreated studio, among the
          reclining heads, etc., there
were many of them. Elongated
          parentheses. Marble.
Bronze. Upward flying.

                    I knew there
          was something dark
amongst those otherworldly
          rotors that
had drawn both Max
          and Mia. An open field
where secrets cannot be
          hidden. I heard
yesterday on the radio
          about how suicide
is more prevalent in
          the spring, something
I pretty much knew. It's
          hypothesized
a person's inner darkness
          is so much
heavier next to the
          foamy blossoms. One's
secret, corrosive
          shame, in the spacious

wind field
        as close as it is
possible to get, in the
        plains,
to the ocean.

        A genius
        thing to catch
the spanking winds
        of the prairie. We've
had winds
        so hard, in March,
on the cusp
        between seasons,
we could
        have powered
New York! But
        that was yesterday,
beautiful day, if windy,
        and today was ugly,
Max was back in
        line. He went home
and talked to his
        parents.

        I've heard
the bird arms
        hurt birds. I've
seen the red lights at
        night, cascading,
warning off low-flying
        planes.

        The relentless soughing
of the turbines,
        apparently,
drives people on the
        neighboring
farms insane. When Max
        speaks of his

suffering, I always
        believe him.
A certain frequency,
        the article
said—not really the
        soughing or
luffing—not audible
        to everyone—a
low, constant,
        ultrasonic
hum underneath;
        anomic,
despondent,
        dysthymic
grinding, that does
        not cease.

RIPTIDE MILAGRO

Late in
            the day
when Lucy
            was packing up
all her things—the
            towels suntan
lotion
            orange
beach umbrella—
            I saw a
gull proudly high up
            in the sky
flashing
            something
silver just
            beneath it
parallel—I'd
            seen this
before
            the proud
conquest
            the victory lap
the brandishing
            of the silver
trophy
            in distended claws
like an underneath
            sidecar
back to the dunes
            to
eat it
            so I had a pretty
good idea
            what I was
looking
            at. I said
Look look
            and she said

I'm trying
            to pack up
all this
            stuff. Her friend Ava
looked for a
            moment polite
half-thrilled as it turned
            slightly adjusted
its flight path.
            Then as it straightened
out I saw it
            in profile
the gull
            flapping forward
and then
            the silver object
in perfect side view
            a definitive
fish-shape. Like
            a piece of
jewelry a fetish
            a filled-in
fish symbol
            like one you might see
on the
            back of a car signifying
a not-so-secret
            allegiance to
Jesus. Or a milagro.

            What would it
be the miracle
            for then? A good
catch or to return
            safely from
the sea? Not
            the well-being
of a breast a leg
            a torso. Perhaps Ava's
mentally

                    ill mother
who fills notebooks
          with hypergraphia—
all gibberish
          Ava says
except a few numbers
          and occasionally
some set prayers. Don
          chimes in
helpfully
          at the dinner
table "Religiosity!" Ava
          is matter-of-fact;
she never
          really knew
her mother
          otherwise.
I will attempt
          similar equanimity. Our
daughter Eleanor's trickery
          abandonment.
On the lam
          in France.
Through which
          lens
are we supposed
          to see
it again?

                    We know
very little. Lithium.
          Pot. Alcohol.
Delusions. Relapse.
          Hapless boyfriend
whose image
          she twists
her mind
          in the service
of. His feckless
          parents. The "less"

words. As in
      "No love
lost."

      Ellen
my elderly father's
      "girl"friend told
us yet another
      story
last night
      about the
sea taking a
      child. His brother
was saved
      by a passerby
but the younger child
      slipped from
the rescuer's grasp
      submerged
and sucked out
      by the riptide. Now all
the parents
      read it—
the helicopters
      all night—in the
paper and are
      cautious. And
Lucy and Ava
      are frolicking there
in that same surf
      every day.

Let it be
      silver fish
Jesus "Ichthys"
      for Ava and
Lucy then for
      Ava's hyper-religious
Mary-worshipping
      mother for

Eleanor—once
        upon a time, she
took to
        Catholicism
like a
        fish to
water. Silver milagro,
        amulet ex-
voto *dije*
        seagull's
souvenir
        of the riptide—
"this is my
        body
which will be
        given up for
you"—about
        to be taken
to a sand
        dune live
and
        devoured
shining.

ON THE MALECÓN

—

Family vacation, Hotel el Pescador, Puerto Vallarta

My *self*
            is like breath on

                        glass.
My name lifts off

            like a cloud
like when you press

            and drag
                        the cursor

the print lifts off
            print, a shadow of the whole phrase

                        wandering.
At night I anchor

            myself down
                        with two winter

blankets—in the tropical
            heat—

                        to keep from floating
up.

            The woman squealed
                        as she was lifted

from the beach
            on the boat-pulled

                        parachute—
a child playing in

— 18 —

                    the surf
                              almost got

tangled
                    in the lines. The operator, holding

                              the woman by
          the shoulder,

                    had to motion the child
away. I saw her rise

                    up up, still
                              pale, with her

mouse-colored
                    ponytail,

                    and squealing, till she
was something in

                    the sky and I wondered
how they would get her

                    down—what maneuver
                              of the little faraway

boat? While up the beach
          beside the Malecón

                              a man sold
                              plastic representations

one could hold
                    on a string like a kite

                    the flapping plastic
                              multicolored umbrella dome

with diamond slit cutouts, like
                the real thing, and the blue-

                or pink-clad plastic
action figure dangling improbably

            below. Such is
                me in paradise—trying

in vain to get coordinates on
            my wayward 18-year-old

                orange-and-red-diaphanous
full-length-sundress

                holed-up-in-a-hotel-room-with-
                    her-French-lover

daughter
                becoming wayward myself

        able only to open my mouth
            and form an O.

O you are hooked on
        pot and sex

O you are but a
        shadow of what I once

                saw you were.
I drift, plastic figure of woman,

        among the palm
fronds over the hotel patio,

        the sound of surf,
the rolling r's of this

country's language.
                    I never knew who I was—

this truth has to be
        told each morning. I

                wake in the dark
trying to assemble

                a lexicon,
                    to make a coherent

line—in the dark
        I scratched

                words on top of each
other on a

            pad by the bed
                "Torture,

torture, torture." At the time
        I thought it

                    brilliant. In the echo chamber
of the stone bathroom

                at night it's possible
to hear other people puking

            besides ourselves—Lucy
                in our room, Eleanor

and Djibril, next door. Barking out their
        chorizo or street-vendor

        taco. What can I possibly
say to my radiant black-haired daughter

about her dissolving
               self, her uncompassionate moods,

the up too up to hear
               the voices of others. The down

               likewise self-absorbed.
What can I say? I am dangling from

          my little parachute
               my parasail, by the

round pool, the stone
          tiles, with the

               yattering children
plastic, buoyant. I drift

          in and out on the sound
               of water.

               A sentence
mislaid,

          a whole phrase
               wandering.

A Fan, a Hair Dryer, an Air-Conditioner: Feast of the Pentecost at Target Supercenter

                    I believe in destiny
        Vee the pedicurist declared—during
            my Mother's Day Express

                        Facial and Pedi Package—
        and I thought
                this might come

                        in handy. Train whistle
        at night
                clack on the tracks

                    shaking me from
        sleep or to go deeper into
                dream, my dead

                        friend Margaret on
        the shallow bottom, one
                fathom deep from the spot

                on the water
        where her love Bob
                had gently laid

                    her and pearls
        for her eyes and leaning
                up in her fox fur stole

                    wafting in the current
        looking regretfully with
                her doughy pocked face

                        at Bob. Or was she just
        dead, inanimate,
                bobbing under

water? You see
I have lost my job
and am going to

another. I take solace
in Target, rolling the
metal cart up and

down the aisles, trying
to remember what the
point was, my mental

list. As soon as I add
"headbands," "telephone"
falls out. A fan, a

hair dryer, an air-conditioner,
Father Dan said this
morning, could be

used to mimic the Holy
Spirit's rushing mighty wind,
or a red ribbon to reflect

the traditional vestments ("cloven
tongues as of fire"). God
forbid, he said. Let this

feast not go the way of the
Paschal, the Nativity.
I don't know why I

love to go to Target
alone, buy random cheap household
items. Hope my mental

list will revive itself—
a wicker magazine
rack to turn upside

                down and put next
to my bed, so as to assist
            the ancient cat

                Sparkling in getting
up and down. Her eyes
            are clouding over and

                she walks like she's
on the deck of a
            trawler. She marks the

                days on the quilt, purrs through
the nights, on the designated
            cat pillow

                beside my resting head.
I can't stand—
            I mean I really can't

                abide—death. Target stays
spanking clean and perky, at least
            the part I can see,

                and I try not to remember
the freight cars I saw
            before coming

                in here, at dusk. One by
one lined up
            like huge white

                refrigerators on their sides, or,
as has often been
            said, coffins. Fired up

                and headed to their
destiny, the trees
            above, boiling

in the stiff wind,
their green tongues
of flame wagging.

The Feast of the Pentecost
fell on Mother's Day. This
must have rankled

Father Dan. The most underrated
Christian holiday with
the most overrated

secular one. I had to drag
Lucy out of bed to
accompany me

to church. I shouted "And
Happy Mother's Day to *you*!"
and she popped up, snatching

her sister's paisley and elephant
print dress and sticking a chopstick
in her hair. Refusing to eat

breakfast and lolling
all over me
during the service.

The mother thing is
winding down. Lucy
prefers her friends

to me much
of the time and Eleanor is basically
not speaking. *Happy Graduation!*

No more rolling
up and down the aisles
of a supercenter

with one girl in the
basket and another, legs dangling, in
the front compartment—

or both girls in the
basket and having to put
the miscellaneous household

goods in their arms
or on their heads.
No one explained

that bit. That they wouldn't
always be there
shining their little

lights, that they would
have somewhere else to go.
Their destinies. Eleanor's latest tangent—

Ghana, Mexico, a "gap"
year. *Please.* And the now-blind cat
who, like the Holy Spirit,

shepherded me
through the pregnancy fourteen
years ago with Lucy

and countless strange nights
since. The multiple-amputee
maple outside

my bedroom window, with the
purple stain on each stump. Not knowing what
my destiny was, I traveled—

jumped around from place to place—
but still there were
always Targets and Walmarts.

                    Father Dan said sometimes
the Holy Spirit calls us
            to do something, maybe

                something we
haven't planned. After Mass, Lucy
        and I walked out

                into the rain under
a navy blue, yellow
        smiley faces-adorned

                umbrella, the tacky
yellow faces well-nigh
        meaningless at this point

                having been so
commercialized, Lucy hugging my arm
        under the blue umbrella sky.

THAT WAS ALL I EVER
KNEW OF NEPAL

I sit in the tub
and watch clouds motor.
After the closed-door

shoutdown with Eleanor,
twelve-year-old Lucy showed
me her poster on Nepal.

The two red triangles
of the Nepalese flag,
symbolizing the Himalayas.

White sun on one.
Cool moon on the
other. Imports: petroleum

products, electricity,
fertilizer. Exports: jute,
leather, clothing, carpet,

hand-hammered tingsha
and singing bowls. Sal wood
obtained in forests, bamboo

and rattan. In her querulous
glitter-glue script: "One of
the poorest countries in

the world." My friend
Megan died there. That
was all I ever knew of Nepal.

I was seventeen. We'd met
for cream-filled donuts from
Ed's Market for breakfast on the

beach in south Jersey. Megan
down from Philly, me from
the suburbs. Her bright winter

skin on the beach in her jeans
and T-shirt. I laughed at her.
We talked about Eric,

her lover. A year later they were
sucked under a truck while motorcycling
in the mountains in Nepal. She'd

told me Eric was her all.
I met him once. She
was funny and kind,

never once offered a critical
word. Eleanor lost a significant
part of her mascara today

to her upper cheek when she
said she was "in love."
Unlike others

she was *actually* in love
and would make her decisions
accordingly. Adventure, even

danger, in Mexico, with her
African/Swiss/French boyfriend. Other exports: grain,
herbal treatments, oils and

pashima. Currency: rupee.
Flag of two pennants also symbolic
of Hinduism and Buddhism.

Blue border, peace and harmony.
Crimson, Nepal's national
color. Brave spirit. The pulse

of the people. Megan had
those qualities. I was too
wrapped up in bimbo-ness to

be able to pin it down. Megan
and Eric died together. Tonight
it's 46, tomorrow it will

be 8. In between, some
violence. In between, some
action. A skyful of scudding

clouds. Eleanor wept real tears
and we administered "tough love."
I said Djibril had to man up

(trying to think of the French
equivalent) and finish high
school. Pay the

price of the year spent
skipping lycée and dealing
hashish. I said nothing

about Megan. I hadn't
seen the poster yet, hadn't
yet shocked the wits

out of Lucy and her friend Ava
by telling them the one
story I knew about their

chosen country. My friend Melinda
Smith from Philly came down
to the shore to visit, fell in love

with Megan's brother, Rob.
I remember her stealthy, labyrinthine
journey into Center City that fall

to the birth control pill doctor so
she could give Rob her flower.
A couple of years later,

after they'd split, she had
a breakdown at Penn.
I hated facing Rob at the beach

the summer after Megan died.
Between that and our shared
history of Melinda I thought

my heart would break. Rob
was a mechanic. He looked
like Arlo Guthrie. Melinda said

all the time how smart
he was. But wasn't it
me, just two weeks ago, after

a twelve-step meeting, advising
the younger man, Jon—
whose beautiful, intent face

(with one curved crease
down each gaunt cheek)
had been coming to me in dream,

whom I thought of also
while awake—about his love life? As
I approached, he stepped back.

I felt like the cellulite
monster. His face, his kind
laughing face, the time he

stopped his pickup in the middle
of Sixth Street in a snowstorm
to speak to me—he said, It's always

a pleasure to see you. Knowing,
I guess, of his effectiveness
          with women. I saw his face

          on the icy highway going to work,
as one commute after another
          the semis fell, taking cars with them.

          Eleanor loves Djibril like a girl.
He's her dove, her coney. I
          know. I do know. "Adventure

          and maybe even danger." I hear
the wind spanking the house. The
          temperature will drop

          forty degrees. Maybe snow.
Jon's knee will never
          be right, from the time

          the police shot him. And
he told me he was worried
          about telling the woman he

          was falling for that he wasn't
from a two-parent family!
          Possible snow

          showers. Severe drop in temperature,
more opportunities for truck
          crackups and the errant, the

          random, the unlucky cars.

RED RUBBER BALL

We slammed the
brakes to keep from
broadsiding the

obnoxious
surfer dudes—one with
his arm dangling

down his passenger-side
door—and instantly
the newly repaired

air conditioning
turns to heat
as we skid to

within an inch
of the sneering faces. The
arrogant arm. The tennis

player, James Blake,
in the *New York Times*
story, so up and coming,

tripped, catapulted into a post
in practice: "The luckiest
thing that happened to me was

breaking my neck."
He wanted to be
with his father who was dying

of stomach cancer and had
refused to let his son
leave the tour. After his

dad died, James Blake
got half-facial paralysis from the
zoster virus (following "extreme

emotional and physical stress"), lost
his ability to play ("the facial nerve . . .
        abuts the hearing and

            balance nerve"), his looks
(who'd just been named "sexiest
        athlete" by *People*

            magazine), this beautiful
man who could've been
        a model, the writer

            said. Eleanor and Lucy
remind me some women wearing
        underwire bras have been

            struck by lightning. There's
my dad, weeping
        as he said goodbye. In the

            porte cochère of Westminster
Canterbury, the old people's
        place. His voice broke

            as he said, "Maybe I'll
see you at Thanksgiving." What
        is left of

            my dad. As he wheels
our paper beach umbrellas,
        boogie boards, and random leftover

            groceries—eggs and soy milk—
taking the key to
        our beach cottage to

            be returned
the next day. So little
        left. His bent

            shape. The objects toppling
from his cart. Other oldies
        scrambling to help him. Eleanor

got out of our miserable
"Love Shack" Rent-a-Wreck
van to assist

but said he'd righted
things, seemed determined.
He asks the same

things over and over.
And his
body is at a tilt. How he

worked when I was
a child. The rototiller,
the Rotary speeches in

front of the dryer. The day job
at the Naval Yard, the night classes,
taken, then taught.

Djibril, Eleanor's boyfriend,
likely understood
the word

"Bitch!" and so on
exchanged in the van
as we got ready

for our 11 p.m. departure.
Struck by lightning in
your underwire, losing

your footing in a
tennis game and slamming
your head into a post or

tearing the arm right off
a surfer dude, trying
to brake. After some months,

James Blake got back
to playing, got back
        his face. "Remarkable

            rally," if not of "next great
American hope"-ness, then
        of patience, of willingness

            to bear sorrow.
The Love Shack swerving,
        possibly tipping over.

            And the hot air
pouring out of
        the "just-repaired"

            air-conditioning vent.
The guy, Tony Cicoria, in the
        Oliver Sacks story,

            after the near-death experience,
after temporary memory
        loss, six weeks or so

            after the event—"I
was talking to my mother.
        There was a little

            bit of rain, thunder
in the distance. My mother
        hung up . . . I

            remember a flash
of light coming out of the
        phone"—when he

            thought the
whole thing
        had blown over,

"developed an
insatiable desire to
listen to piano music," then

started to hear
music in his head, had to teach
himself how to

write it down. He became
"very spiritual" and read everything
about near-death experiences

and high-voltage electricity
he could find. "Next thing
I remember, I was flying

backwards. Then . . . I was
flying forwards . . . I saw
my own

body on the ground.
I said to myself, 'Oh shit,
I'm dead.'"

The afternoon
sun laying its sharp blade
on the blue

water, the sand.
Eleanor's question under
the beach umbrella: "How

will I live
in Africa?" The sun on the horizon. "Red
rubber ball," like the song

from the Sixties.
Driving down
Shore Drive in the Love Shack

at 11 p.m. after
saying goodbye to my
        fragile decrepit father. It's like

                my head
will blow
        apart. Eleanor, I don't know

        how life would be
with Djibril in Africa.
        "The impact was so violent that Blake's racket . . .

        looked . . . as if a sharp-toothed
animal had bitten into it . . . .
        In short,

        Blake was extremely
lucky . . . ." The sun bouncing
        on the earth's rim.

        "A straight
shot, with
        its downward pressure

        on the spinal cord,
could have caused paralysis."
        "Red Rubber

        Ball," the Top 40 hit,
Monkees' rendition,
        I sunbathed to, on the

        Jersey shore, in my
wannabe bandana bikini. Then bang bop
        it's . . . .

ANNOUNCEMENT:
THE THEME OF TONIGHT'S PARTY HAS BEEN CHANGED

We switched the theme
     of the party
from Tropical
     Night to
Old Dog Vestibular
     Disease but
didn't have time
     to get the
word out so
     Porter, Eric,
and a couple
     of students
came in straw hats and
     board shorts, sunglasses
propped on their wiry
     heads.
Willa had a
     grass skirt. The
sick dog was featured
     in a cage
up near the
     front door. She
had finished
     seizing. I saw
to that with
     an "injectable"
of dexamethasone
     wheedled from
Dr. Stroud that
     afternoon. But
she was
     still panting
and listing and
     not allowed
to stand. The guests
     had to maneuver

around her
            to get to
the San Pelegrino, wine,
            and beer. She
barked once,
            sharply, seeing
a person thieving
            from the
cooler.

            The ailment is sometimes
            less pejoratively
called
            Canine Vestibular
Disease. I loved
            her for refusing
to be stashed
            in the back
seat of the Volvo
            as she
usually is
            for Don's visiting
writer parties. (Many
            times, ignored,
I've wished
            to hang there
with her.) For
            tonight, insisting
on putting her (mostly)
            mute self
front and center.

                        Two
            people
buttonholed me
            drunk. It
took me a minute
            to figure
out that their
            confidently
delivered
            statements

were nonsense. They
        were sentences,
they were on
        topic. With Helene,
it was the light
        gleam of sweat
on her forehead
        her upper lip
her erotic slit-eyed gaze at
        our guest of
honor, which could
        not have been
more inappropriate—
        but this
is the only thing
        some people can
think of in terms
        of poetic
"intensity." While
        she drank
him in seductively
        tilting her
chin up slightly
        she made
an utterly insipid
        statement
about his use
        of tetrameter (which
he'd already explained
        was deeply
personal—*the man
        writes poems
to God!*) and
        hers of the
sonnet. SNORE. And
        her students'
resistance to
        the use of form.
Double snore.
        The other

person nailed
me by the mirror,
            kept repeating,
Sally looks so young!,
            referring to
the dog. I said,
            Yeah, well,
she's not, and then,
            finally,
I don't think
            we have
much time left
            with her.
I wanted
            to say she
was recently groomed
            at the kennel. That
she was simply
            clean, not
young. I wanted
            to say,
Look in
            her eyes. There's
a film, like iridescence
            on a puddle.
She's practically
            blind. Look
at her hind
            legs. They're
sticks, constantly
            flying akimbo.

I've been those
            people. Helene, with
her head thrown back
            to imbibe
the honoree.
            During
my high-slut
            phase, I had

scant knowledge of
         poetry and certainly
wasn't teaching
         a class. That
was the only
         difference. I hated
her avaricious
         sweaty sexual
moon face
         though.
                        Paul, by
the mirror,
         a Crate and Barrel
special, improbably
         decorated
with coat hooks,
         going on about
Sally's "youthful
         appearance," wasn't I *him*?
Recently? Complaining
         he'd been
passed over for a
         job by
an inside candidate
         who *had*
no pubs—and then was
         never
notified. I joined in,
         loudly exclaiming
I'd been on unemployment
         a year and
a half, and was
         now, at this point,
an honorary canine.

                        I wanted
         to think
of something else, seeing
         Willa in her
grass skirt, besides

the times
she insulted me
that year
I held the "visiting
position." I blocked
out the day
she kind of
tried to make
it up to me
in the Marsh
parking lot. Telling
me about her
sister, sick
in Ireland, and her recent
trip to
Cambodia. Without a
direct apology,
it didn't
count.
She
stuck her foot
out once at
some reception, in
front of
a bunch
of people,
and giggled maliciously
when I nearly
tripped. Another
time, she sighed
loudly when
I turned up
in front of her in
an auditorium,
as if my height
was going to be
some kind
of insurmountable
barrier to her
view (I kept

thinking, I'm not
          even tall
from the waist up).

                    The afternoon
          before the party
I crawled into
          the cage
with Sally
          when she
was violently
          shaking.
I started
          giving orders.
First I got
          Don to go
get the oral
          prednisone, and when,
after a couple
          of hours, she still
did not
          improve, and Don
was no longer
          there to help,
I called around
          for the needle. I had
to leave her at home
          in the crate
for about 15 minutes
          to go pick it
up. Every
          second, I thought
of my ill
          father, at
a similar
          stage, with his
Parkinson's tremor
          and disequilibrium.
His Sally-like
          determination,

valor, courtesy.

                    We haven't
            had to use
the ramp to get
            her up and
down the front
            porch steps
since the
            night of the
party, the night
            of the last
attack. It had been
            hours and I knew
she had to
            pee. I lured
her down the retractable
            ramp with
half a dog
            biscuit in
my free hand and my
            daughter Lucy
guiding her
            feeble rear
end walking down
            the steps at
her side. A few people
            were arriving
and squeezing through
            on what was
left of the stairs
            to get into
the party where
            the real thing,
whatever that was—
            the greasy
overtures, the
            florid missing-the-
mark red-in-the-face
            remarks,

snubbing
     and being snubbed,
intricate status
     updates
and assessments—
     was going on.
               My
daughter had laid
     out the platters.
Alternating
     leaves of radicchio
and endive around
     the rim of
one, with the bleu cheese
     dip forming
the hub cap. Bowls of
     tortilla chips, mounds
of Milanos. Such
     are the reliable
forms. A white-frosted
     cake with our
visiting poet's name
     written in
blue script between
     red rose blossoms
on the top. All
     things
requiring a higher
     intelligence
than Sally's. I walked her
     down the street,
farther and farther from
     the house lights,
into the dampness,
     her spirit
steady, her corporeal
     self swinging
uncertainly
     from side
to side.

"Die High"

Harold said
the Marine motto was,
        though I don't

        think it appears
on any recruitment
        literature. Then,

        a storm, negative
ions, at last.
        We were all insane

        from the heat. I stood
in the scuffed cement portico of
        a student

        rental. "The Brothel,"
it said in
        neat block lettering

        on the mailbox
with a two-period
        ellipsis

        after. A boy/man
in a buzz cut
        opened the door

        and offered
to let me in. I
        saw several men's

        pairs of shoes
and one pair of black
        baby doll high heels

                    heaped on the carpet
near the door. I ended
        up with

                a wooden chair
on the cement
        slab watching

                the rain
cascade
        and surge

                down the
street, hoping my garden
        was getting

                drenched,
hoping my hanging
        plants

                at home
on the porch were
        getting "hydrated"

                osmotically. I read an article
in Sunday's paper
        called "Addictive

                Personality? You Might
Be a Leader" in which
        it's posited

                "risk-takers" are
risk-takers because they
        actually get high

                less easily than
"normal" people do—
        and need

more—and
hence keep seeking.
My only

risk,
running
in the fomenting

thunderstorm.
A high hot wind,
frenzied trees,

and a big wall
cloud from which
a tornado could

have extended
its slender foot. On
the bridge,

I took
off my hat with
its metal button

on the top and moved
my bobby pins
to the waist band

of my shorts. Linking
lightning strikes
to thunder

with Hail Mary's.
Looking frantically
to make sure

I was *not*
the tallest
thing.

When
the lightning and
thunder pretty

much coincided
and the rain
got bad-heavy

I stopped in
the portico. I've gotten
good at timing

these things,
as in my bartender days
when I could

hold a bottle vertical
and pour and know whether
one shot, shot and

a half, or two
had gotten into the glass. A
student of

climax.

* * *

"Die high,"
Harold said
in his life story.

But now
he's clean
and sober. He's

crawling
the walls half
the time—more than

half, I know.
ADD, Type A, ADHD,
         anxious, depressed,

             sex-obsessed,
etc., etc. This is what the dead singer
         Amy Winehouse

             could not
get to, the daily
         grinding of

             sobriety. Not her
preferred
         destination.

             I didn't
wear any makeup
         to the rheumatology

             floor; I wanted
Dr. J. to see the
         allergic, migrainous

             shiners under
my eyes, every sign
         of the long

             messed-up
nights, the slow, excruciating
         mornings.

             I even wrote
her a two-page
         single-spaced

             recitation of
my symptoms and
         itemized them together

in groups
to show the clusters—like
migraine/IBS/fibromyalgia,

hypothyroid/mood
swings/sensitivity to cold fronts,
GERD/

hiatal
hernia/alcoholism. And oh
yes, R.A.—fodder

for some
Debbie Downer monologue
on SNL, "trying to fix

the mess in my
head with the mess
in my head." I don't

know if she
read it (because
she had an

annoying resident
there first, whom I summarized
everything for and gave

the list to), but she
got it. She said, Got it
Got it Got it

and listed
what she would
do were she

my doc—and
of course I stated
on the spot

that she was. A perfect
slim cute Michelle
Pfeiffer-type, in a

fitted print cotton
dress, with contemporary
glasses. She said

I want you off Tylenol
and onto this one—
it's got a tiny bit

of anti-depressant,
holding up her fingers
in a pinch. Magic

bullet, Tramadol!
When I got home,
I looked it up

and read the
warning. "You should not take
this medication

if you have
ever been
addicted to drugs

or alcohol."

* * *

Amy Winehouse
was "famously blunt
in her assessment of

her peers,
once describing
Dido's sound as

'background music — the
background to death'
and saying of pop

princess Kylie Minogue,
'she's not an artist . . .
she's a pony.'" God love

her. Apart
from my horse
habit—Blue

ducking the jump
and me flying
over—my

sleep thing,
and, well, the sex
thing, I

am straight as
a German Baptist woman
from up north

in a starchy
translucent
voile cap. So tired

I live in the
twilight zone, can't
get in the

swing
of anything.

* * *

Zoey, my new

calico
cat, now that
my daughters

and husband
aren't at home,
            gets on my chest

            at night—I pull
up the covers
            so she won't

            cut me with her
claws when she kneads me. She
            drools

            from her mouth
or her nose, hard to tell
            which—a clear

            drop dangles
from her tiny
            septum. She purrs

            loud. She sometimes
nudges me
            for one second

            on the lips
with her pink lip or
            puts

            her paw
practically around
            my neck.

            This morning
when I was talking to
            Felicia, my neighbor,

            about my flooded
basil planter, Zoey jumped
            on the

porch
with a stricken bird in her
jaws. Striped wings

splayed as if
in flight. Determined
to show

me what her clever
mouth was
doing at that point!

Wow! I screamed,
gestured for
Felicia

to give me her
rake so I could
break it up

but Felicia was
still on the conversation about
the planter. Zoey

leapt off
the porch, crouched
under a bush

and Dieu merci,
after some scuffling, and me screaming
"No!," the bird flew straight

away, patterned
wings extended, and across
the street. My little

lover, who
kisses me at night.

* * *

                    I was
          crushed to

                    read on the internet
how Tramadol, "synthetic
          opioid,"

                    was "addictive,"
"habit-forming,"
          well-nigh impossible

                    to withdraw from—
and the "black box"
          warning about

                    how it could not
be dispensed
          to past or present addicts/

                    alcoholics. Kept trying
to figure out
          how to fudge. Maybe

                    I was just
a pretend addict/alcoholic,
          that kind of thing. Then

                    thinking of my
friends, with their
          long, long

                    lists of psychotropic
drugs and painkillers. The
          ones who can

                    no longer write,
fuck, feel.
          It reminded me

of 1980 after
Kurt left
me; I was severely

anemic (didn't
notice it) and quite thin. Dr. C.
took one

look at me and gave me
Valium (I mean daily). When
I said, six months

in, I was
worried about being
addicted, he

gave me Librium.
The withdrawal from
that was hell—alone

in a beach house
with my *mother!* (Thank God
for alcohol.) Our sessions

consisted
of him talking
about "Monty" Cliff

and "Jimmy" Dean.
I learned later (how
could I have

missed it?) he
was a "closet homosexual." Plus
he came

from a family
that practically owned
the state. Those were days

I wanted never
to revisit—my mid-
twenties—

but it was
"back to black" again
and again. This morning,

for example,
something feathered and
other

struggled in my
mouth. A sudden snap of
wings as it

escaped. Then
the scumbled sky,
lightning on the bridge.

POEM IN A BOTTLE

The signs I have
to say weren't that good.
                    Over the loudspeaker,
announcements about
                    the mechanic dicking
around on the previous flight
                    to Detroit, the young
girl/woman from Georgia
                    catty-corner to me
being overly pleasant
                    and friendly, in the
waiting area,
                    as if we'd
already arrived
                    in heaven, who said
she'd never flown before.
                    She watched my
stuff twice
                    when I went to the
bathroom—more
                    airport naiveté—and when
she first sat down she
                    asked the big, pot-bellied
guy on her other side if he
                    was bored and wanted
a game! (I guess she had
                    an electronic
something.) Is there
                    anybody left on the
planet that innocent? There was the
                    de-icing just before
we took off—sloshing
                    of the wings with
some kind of noxious
                    pale-green chemical
antifreeze. I said I thought
                    the temperature

was supposed to be
           well above
freezing, but the guy
           in the
seat next to me
           who let me sit on
the aisle
           said there was sleet
on the window.
           Then there was the God-
awful takeoff
           during which I pulled
the white plastic rosary
           from my pocket
and started mouthing
           the prayers, trying to
discipline myself
           to not skip part 1-b
which is "Blessed are
           you among women
and the fruit of
           your womb
Jesus." I kept
           wanting to skip through
from "Hail Mary, Full of Grace" to the
           "Pray for us now and at
the hour of our
           death" part. Then the
layer of turbulence
           right after takeoff
that made the
           plane feel like a
pair of metal pancake
           spatulas rubber-banded
together, flapping
           in a high wind.
There was the
           "captain" in her
hat with her
           tangled blond

hair at the
          bagel stand before
takeoff, very disturbing
          that 1) she could not
comb her hair (indicator
          of a rough night?)
2) she was mortal
          enough to eat a
bagel and might
          possibly be flying
the plane with
          dirty teeth. I saw
her striding toward
          the gate in her
impeccable
          clothes and shaggy
hair—wasn't
          she required
to wear a ponytail
          or hairnet or something
in the event of
          challenging circumstances
requiring athleticism?
          My shaky dad
saying goodbye at
          the front door of
Westminster Canterbury where
          the driver, "Sylvia," had
come to pick me up.
          Trying to smile at
me with his stiff
          grimace, the scar on
his upper lip from melanoma
          surgery, to lift my
suitcase into the trunk
          of her dark
blue coupe with
          his tremulous
hand. There was the
          laundry list

of loose ends
        I'd gone over
with him the night
        before: 1) give
up driver's license, find
        rides to church
and the pool at Cox, 2) find
        helper for dressing
specifically
        buttons and 3) extend
power of attorney
        to Doug and me
in addition to John
        in the event
he might become incapacitated—
        or that one
or both of them might
        be "indisposed"
and unable to answer
        the phone. And
his going over
        again the details
of the car "incident" that
        had prompted the person
in the other car to call
        the DMV. The location
of the will, the life
        insurance policies,
and so on. There was finding
        last night
that photo—as soon
        as I went back
into the box
        to try to find it
to keep it, it was gone, of
        course. A tiny black-and-white
from the 50s, my father,
        and me, at about
age six, sitting before
        two bushels

of apples.

       We had gotten up
past that layer
       in which the
whole dinky plane
       rattled,
up into the sun. I started
       thinking
maybe I shouldn't
       have been so
snobbish and bored by
       the mindless chatter
in the ante-
       room to heaven. Then
yelling ten times at the
       ignoramuses
on the jetway,
       ostentatiously
carrying their ungainly bags
       of skis, about how Indiana,
nearly all of it,
       is in the
Eastern Time Zone;
       one of the overgrown
adolescent middle-aged
       jock skier types
had declared
       self-confidently
the border of the Eastern
       Time Zone
ran right down the middle
       of Indiana—*not*.
There was my hunched-over
       father, his labored
gait, in his maroon
       windbreaker,
stuttering his goodbye.
       In the picture my father
with his shy smile

and good head of
hair was looking at
        the camera. My hair
was short and my bangs
        were cut
straight across. We must
        have been in Linvilla
Orchard. I remember
        the cider press, and
the smell of the cider
        in the big glass
jugs we brought
        home. My hand is on his
arm and I'm leaning my head
        on his shoulder.
Like I was tired
        of the great harvest
I myself desired.

Voodoo Lou's Office Voodoo Kit

"You can give someone a headache by taking and turning
their picture upside down."
                                        Louisiana Voodoo

Thirty-eight per cent
of poets are bipolar, says Donald Hall,
poet, who seems to me

in his memoir to be somewhat
dysthymic—but his wife, Jane Kenyon,
certainly fit the bill. I've

waited a long time
for this mediocre spring to
get off the ground, and

I deserve my high. She
said. Before the Easter Vigil,
I bought these things for

Lucy's Easter basket:
Double fudge egg, 60% cacao Cadbury
bar, four dark-blue-foil-wrapped

dark chocolate Lindor
truffles. Two fuzzy yellow chicks, one that
walks when you wind it

up. "Japanese Garden in a
Box," "Therapist in a Box," "Chakras,"
and "Office Voodoo Kit." I ended up

keeping the last two
for myself. Not that
I would ever perform

voodoo on those people.
I sympathize with Hillary Clinton. After being
edged out, but still

retaining her constituency,
her power base, she
could not do/say

the right thing. The Obama-kins
stared at her
through narrowed

eyes. They simply wanted
her to blow up. Likewise, me
on my visit to my

old job, from which I was
extracted by a contingent
of men. In a word. Bipolar

is not my word. Happy
that spring finally turned up,
yes. High about that,

yes. My daughter, possibly
considerably more definitely in the
bipolar direction, flying under

the radar (mine, and I hope
all of the Mexican troublesome elements')
on her driving trip to Acapulco,

in the car that I forbade
her to take more than an hour
out of her Michoacán town,

Sahuayo. Of course. She flies
over me like Evel Knievel. Like I'm just an
aggravating mattress in

the road. So, I repeat,
voodoo is not for me. I am MUCH too
wimpy for that. The people

on the other side of
the equation, however—I can't say
for sure about them.

I bought the kit, gulped
down some dinner at Panera with Don,
attended twelve-step meeting (at

which angel Steve,
whose wife died of cancer two
years ago, said I was important

to him, he always liked
what I said—the OPPOSITE of being
winced at like a random particle

with a "blow up—*combust*—
now" squint, as I was the recipient
of at my

former employer's
last week. God bless Steve who kept
me alive).

At the Vigil Mass, Father Dan
positively *drenched* me with holy water
after that bit where

we the congregation
denounced Satan and all his works
promised to reject

the "glamour of evil."
He came down the aisle brandishing
his fat shaving brush

and whacked us
with the water of life. As he
does every year. I had

long since
started sobbing. That was when
the choir led us

in the Litany of Saints. Holy Mary.
Pray for us. Holy Mother of God.
Pray for us. Holy Virgin

of virgins. Saint Michael. Saint Gabriel.
Saint Raphael: Patrons of Policemen,
Communications Workers,

Travelers and Healers, respectively.
All ye holy Angels
and Archangels.

Pressure in
both directions, apparently, led, in Haiti and
elsewhere, to the marriage

of the Vodou Loa to the
the usurper Catholic saints. For example, St. Peter,
keeper of the keys,

transmutes to
Papa Limba, Laba, guardian of crossroads,
gates, entrances to villages.

St. Peter, St. Peter, open the door,
I'm callin' you, come to me! Papa Legba, open the
gate for me.
Incense choking

the air. Father Dan,
at the head of the
procession, swinging the fuming

censer. Nicholas Hughes, eulogized
today in the *Times,* lived in a log house
overlooking the Brooks Range,

wrote scholarly
treatises about the fish of the snowy
rivers of Alaska, took underwater

pictures of the salmon, the
grayling, ate the "homely turbot"—
but hated academia.

His depression and
"office politics" didn't mix, small
wonder. He recently

resigned his associate
professorship—more recently, by the
aid of a thin

cord in his workshop,
his life. I hadn't been
able to visualize curly-haired, handsome

Ethan's face from two days after
his death, through his funeral,
which I didn't attend,

through two months of
frigid, gelid, unrelenting
winter, until about a week

ago—when I sat in the chair,
in the particular corner in the particular
meeting room, where he had sat the last

time I saw him. Then, there
he was, complaining in his
lovely, verbal, lawyerly

sentences about his bizarrely
schizoid childhood religious training or
lack thereof. I remember, his

Protestant father had him
baptized and his Jewish mother
was livid. It was another of

his disquisitions that ended
with this implicit conclusion, "And this is why
I cannot live on the

planet." That night, I had to
get back to Lucy and did not
stay to talk with him (did I

try to second-guess that
in the rain on my way
to the car?), but Mike told

me later he did, at length,
and I had stopped Ethan
another night, a few weeks before, in the

parking lot outside the Lutheran
Church where we'd had our
Saturday night meeting. I said

something like, I like
what you said. Believe me you're not
the only one who feels

as you do. Or, you're
not alone. He smiled, greeted me, got
in his car. He had his sponsee, young

blue-eyed pompadoured
Andrew, with him, as always, who
was in a real make or break

place after Ethan shot himself
but seems to be making it. I
saw him the other night

and he said he
has another sponsor now, also
             tart and to the point, and was on

                   the mend. Now that Ethan
is back and hanging in my vision
             just on the visor of

                   my eyelashes, I wish
his name was still
             on everyone's lips. Nicholas

                   Hughes' suicide went
by in a hush. No one wanted to offend
             the memory of the son

                   of two famous poets,
one a famous suicide; virtual stepson of
             Assia, another

                   famous suicide
six years later who took his half-sister
             with her. He was clear

                   of voodoo, sounded like,
giving or getting, but was disturbed
             by the infighting between

                   his sister Frieda and their
stepmother Carol on the subject of their
             father's estate. Apropos of

                   nothing, I read last night
on the internet about a woman
             with a "pale, milky-white,

                   translucent third arm,"
that scratched her real neck. It appeared
             a few days after a

stroke and it seems
she could retrieve it
when needed. The MRI proved

the brain perceived
it and her eyes saw it. Easter Sunday, and Lucy
is trying not to think

about her wandering sister,
who's loose in Mexico, whom we cannot
find (at this moment—presumably

she will call?). She takes
the yoga mat out to the yard
and does salutations to the sun

in the real sun. She carries
her Therapist in a Box and her Japanese Meditation
Garden, replete with tiny

tray and sand. I'm off to
my writing office with a tiny pebble for each
chakra, and attendant book,

and my miniature voodoo doll
with pins. One gender per side
and quadrants

marked as in a butcher's
map of cuts of beef,
areas labeled "Lost Contract," "Tight

Deadlines," "Big Bonus," "Fired
Without Cause," and so on. Which
I have no intention of

using. That kind of thing
would boomerang to me
I'm sure. Among other

reasons. Like that it's
Easter, for example. I do have
a headache though as I did

the whole campus visit,
"guest teaching" at my former
place of employ last week. So I'm

wondering if someone
is holding my photo
upside down

with ill intent. Maybe
sticking a pin
in. Or jabbing it with

a pale fish-like para-arm.
Is Facebook a kind of
voodoo, I'm starting to wonder?

All the little images
hanging two-dimensionally
in one direction. Like

little front sides
of the moon (I know Michael from
the Seventies looks

like hell in his
picture and I wondered if
he'd become an

alcoholic). Not
willing to let anyone see
behind. But suggestive of

a whole life, mythology. Maybe
somebody is working on
me that way. Just to be

reductive, I will tell
you the truth. My mother did
not wish me well.

Or maybe some of
the time she did, which is the reason
I thrived as well

as I did. Lots of headaches
though. Like the bad one of the last
week. The week before.

She was vindictive,
my normally undramatic father has said. At
one point, not long before

her cancer diagnosis, she told him
she was suicidal. My father
was stunned. In Sahuayo

we climbed the hill
to the statue of Jesus and the underground
sanctuary for José Sánchez del Río,

the martyr. Eleanor and Djibril were
with us. Eleanor had that
smile she has when she's

with him. I stopped
in to see the martyr's body, or the
representation of same,

and to buy scapulars and prayer cards
from the nice woman. May Father Dan's holy
water reach her wherever

she is. And my daughter (who
was once a Eucharistic
minister in Father

Dan's church). And Lucy
in the yard, in Downward-facing
Dog. All ye holy orders

of blessed Spirits. Pray for us. Sancte
Joánnes Baptista, pray for us. St. Peter
with your keys,

Papa Limba, Laba, Papa
Legba, *open the gate*. Hermes,
god of the crossroads,

where Nicholas Hughes sits
at a potter's wheel; god of travel
flying above my daughter

on those Mexican
switchbacks, protect her. Marie
Leveau, 1830s New Orleans

Voodoo queen
and Li Grand Zombi, ten-foot-long
jewel-studded cobra, whom

she carries in her abundant
black hair, perform your miracles.
Heal us, believers.

Sancte Paule. All ye
Holy Innocents. . . . All ye holy Martyrs, José
Sánchez del Río, who had

the bottom of his feet sheared off
(you can see it in his
glass casket—that couldn't

be his real body!—in the
sanctuary) for refusing to renounce
his Catholic

faith. All ye holy doctors. All
ye Holy Monks and Hermits. Orate pro
nobis. All ye Holy, Righteous,

and Elect of God. Marie
and Paul; Peter, Papa Limba,
from all evil

deliver us. From all deadly
sin, from sudden and unrepentant
death. Mary, Holy Mother of

God, Virgin of virgins. Take Ethan
by the hand. From the peril of
earthquake, fire, and

flood. *Haiti. Nicholas.*
From pestilence, famine
and battle, from everlasting

damnation. *New Orleans.*
By the mystery of the
Holy Incarnation, Good Lord,

deliver us. Be unto us a
tower of strength. Adho Mukha
Svanasana, Downward-facing

Dog. According to the tiny
Easter basket book, it is recommended for the
relief of fatigue and headaches,

strengthens the third and fourth
chakras (solar plexus
and heart). I'd like

to be let up from my head-down
position, from lightning and tempest,
from anger and hatred, and all

uncharitableness. All ye
holy orders of blessed Spirits,
please.

ACKNOWLEDGMENTS

Thanks to the editors of the following journals, in which these poems, sometimes in different versions, first appeared: *Alaska Quarterly Review:* "'Die High'"; *Blackbird:* "That Was All I Ever Knew of Nepal"; *Cimarron Review:* "Poem in a Bottle"; *The Laurel Review:* "Red Rubber Ball," "Genius of the Prairie: Benton County Wind Farm"; *Michigan Quarterly Review:* "Deliver Us from Evil"; *New Ohio Review:* "Announcement: The Theme of Tonight's Party Has Been Changed"; *Notre Dame Review:* "Voodoo Lou's Office Voodoo Kit"; *Prairie Schooner:* "On the Malecón," "Riptide Milagro"; and *The Southern Review:* "A Fan, a Hairdryer, an Air Conditioner: Feast of the Pentecost at Target Supercenter."

For their encouragement and valuable editorial advice, I would like to thank Suzanne Cleary, Wyn Cooper, Hilene Flanzbaum, Mary Leader, David Dodd Lee, Alessandra Lynch, and Daniel Morris. Special thanks to Donald Platt.

I am indebted to Yaddo, the Virginia Center for the Creative Arts, St. James Cavalier Centre for Creativity in Valletta, Malta (through the VCCA International Exchange), and the Ragdale Foundation for residencies that aided in the completion of this book. A fellowship from the National Endowment for the Arts provided support during the writing of some of these poems.

Heartfelt thanks to Melora Griffis for the use of her painting *Hollywood* on the book's cover, and thank you, also, to the judges of the Juniper Prize competition and University of Massachusetts Press.

THE
JUNIPER
PRIZE

This volume is the 37th recipient of the
Juniper Prize for Poetry presented annually
by the University of Massachusetts Press
for a volume of original poetry. The prize is
named in honor of Robert Francis (1901–1987),
who lived for many years at Fort Juniper,
Amherst, Massachusetts.